The Bremen Town Musicians

A Tale about Working Together

Retold by Susan Kueffner
Illustrated by Dominic Catalano

Famous Fables™

Reader's Digest Young Families

Once there was an old donkey who lived on a farm. When he was younger, he had been as strong as an ox, but after years of pulling the farmer's cart to market he was weak and weary. He liked to spend his days munching hay and feeling the warm sunshine on his back. It felt so good, he'd often throw back his head and sing out, *"Hee-haw, hee-haw!"*

One day, he overheard his master tell the mistress of the house, "All he does is eat, eat, eat! And what a lot of noise! It's time to sell him for a donkey who can pull his weight."

The donkey didn't wait to hear another word. That night, he decided to run away to Bremen where he could sing for his supper. *"Hee-haw!"* he said. "I'll be a musician! That's the life for me!"

Along the way, the donkey met a downtrodden dog. "*Bow wow!*" barked the dog. "Where are you off to, my friend?"

"I'm going to town to sing for my supper. You come, too!" said the donkey.

"Don't mind if I do," said the dog. "That's the life for me!"

Farther along, they met a castaway cat. "*Meow!*" mewed the cat. "Where are you off to, my friends?"

"We're going to town to sing for our supper. You come, too!" said the dog and the donkey.

"Don't mind if I do," said the cat. "That's the life for me!"

Down the road, they met a ragtaggle rooster. "*Cock-a-doodly-doo!*" crowed the rooster. "Where are you off to, my friends?"

"We're going to town to sing for our supper. You come, too!" said the cat, the dog, and the donkey.

"Don't mind if I do," said the rooster. "That's the life for me!"

So with a *hee-haw, a bow wow, a meow,* and a *cock-a-doodly-doo,* they set off through the wood to Bremen. It wasn't long before they spied a house in the distance.

When they got to the house, the donkey stood on his hind legs and peered inside. A lovely aroma wafted through the window.

"*Doodly-doo!*" said the rooster. "What doooo you see?"

"*Haw, haw!*" said the donkey. "Fragrant stew, apples and plums, a lovely salmon, and golden corn! And a band of robbers counting their gold!"

"What should we do?" asked the cat, licking her chops.

"Sing for our supper, of course!" said the dog.

They took their places. The donkey stood beside the window. The dog climbed on the donkey's back. The cat climbed on the dog's back, and the rooster flew to the top. The donkey stomped his foot. At the signal, they all began to sing.

"Hee-haw! Bow wow! Meow! Cock-a-doodly-doo!
Bow! Haw! Haw! Cock-a-doodly-dee! Hee! Hee!
Meooooowww! Owwww! Wow! Diddle-dee!
Boo-wee! Haw! Haw!"

Ooo, wee! What a racket it was!

The robbers stopped to stare at the four-headed monster baring its claws and making a most horrid sound outside their window. They dropped their forks with a clatter and a clang! Frantically stumbling over each other in their haste, they ran out the back door into the night.

Our four friends sat down at the table to feast on the treats and tidbits, the likes of which they had never seen before. They munched and chomped and chewed and licked and pecked and gobbled, until they could gobble no more. Then they settled down for a good night's sleep.

Far off in the forest, the robbers saw the light in the house go out. Was the monster gone? They sent a scout back to find out.

The robber tiptoed into the house. It was dark as cinders. He saw the cat's red eyes aglow by the fireplace. Mistaking them for dying embers, he blew on them for more light.

The cat leaped up, hissing and spitting, and clawed his arms. The donkey awoke and kicked the intruder with his hind legs. The dog bit his ankle, and the rooster shrieked and flew at his head!

They so frightened the robber that he ran all the way back into the wood. After that, he and his band of thieves were never seen in those parts again.